Patricia MacLachlan • Illustrations by Amanda Shepherd

Who
Loves
Me?

JOANNA COTLER BOOKS
An Imprint of HarperCollins Publishers

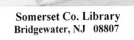

Library of Congress Cataloging-in-Publication Data
MacLachlan, Patricia.
Who loves me? / by Patricia MacLachlan ; illustrations by Amanda Shepherd.— 1st ed.
p. cm.
Summary: At bedtime, a cat in the window reassures a little girl that family members, friends, her
dog, and even her brother love her.
ISBN 0-06-027976-1 — ISBN 0-06-027977-X (lib. bdg.)
[1. Love—Fiction. 2. Interpersonal relations—Fiction. 3. Cats—Fiction.] I. Shepherd, Amanda, ill. II. Title.
PZ7.M2225Wj 2005   2004000697
[E]—dc22

Typography by Alicia Mikles   1 2 3 4 5 6 7 8 9 10   ❖   First Edition

This is for Emily.
With love.
—P.M.

For Dilys—
mentor, hero, friend
—A.S.

"Who loves me?" asks the little girl. It is nighttime. Moonlight falls across her bed.

"Your mother loves you," says the cat in the window. "She planted you a garden of white lilies. They shine like lights in the dark."

"Who loves me?" asks the little girl again.

"Your papa loves you," says the cat. "He built you a wooden playhouse with blue shutters and a stone path."

"And a window box of pansies," says the little girl.

"That too," says the cat.

"And your brother loves you."

"Sometimes I don't know that," says the little girl.

"Well, he does," says the cat.

"Your grandmothers love you," says the cat. "They love you even when you're cranky."

"Mostly when I'm not," says the little girl.

"Your grandfathers teach you about the fish

in the pond," says the cat.

"And about dancing," says the little girl.
"And dancing," echoes the cat.

"Your cousins play hide-and-seek with you," says the cat.

"We whisper secrets," says the little girl.

"Your friends love you," says the cat.

"Sometimes we argue," says the little girl.

"That's all right," says the cat. "They love you anyway."

"What about the dog? The dog loves you," says the cat.
"I feed him treats," says the little girl.
"He would love you even if you didn't," says the cat.

"Who else loves me?" asks the little girl. She smiles. She knows the answer.

"I love you," says the cat. "I brought you a mouse once."

"I remember," says the little girl, yawning.
"I let it go."

"So you did," says the cat.

"That mouse loves you, too."

But the little girl didn't hear that. She was fast asleep.

The cat leaped onto the bed and curled up under her chin.

The little girl dreamed.
The cat dreamed.
Slowly, the moon moved away.